SCIENCE WITH
WATER

Helen Edom
Designed by Jane Felstead
Illustrated by Simone Abel
Consultant: Frances Nagy (Primary Science Adviser)

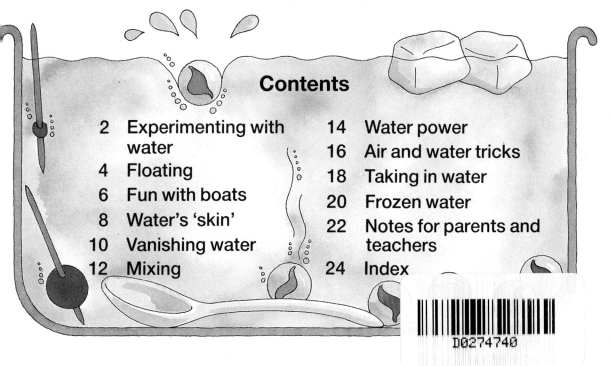

Contents

2 Experimenting with water

4 Floating

6 Fun with boats

8 Water's 'skin'

10 Vanishing water

12 Mixing

14 Water power

16 Air and water tricks

18 Taking in water

20 Frozen water

22 Notes for parents and teachers

24 Index

Experimenting with water

Water behaves in some surprising ways. The experiments in this book will help you find out about them.

Things you need

You can do all the experiments with everyday things. Here are some useful things to collect.

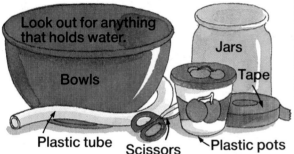

Look out for anything that holds water.

Jars

Bowls

Tape

Plastic tube   Scissors   Plastic pots

Being a scientist

Read what you have to do carefully. See if you can guess what might happen before you try an experiment.

Science notebook

Watch closely to see if you were right. Write or draw everything you notice in a notebook.

Changing shape

Try doing these things to start finding out about water.

Pour water on some hard ground outside. Pour more water into a small jar. Does the water make the same shape?

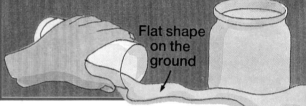

Flat shape on the ground

Looking at the top

Lid on bottle

Level table

The top of the water goes level like a table-top.

Try gently shaking a bottle half-full of water. What happens to the top, or surface, of the water? Let the bottle stand. What happens to the top now?

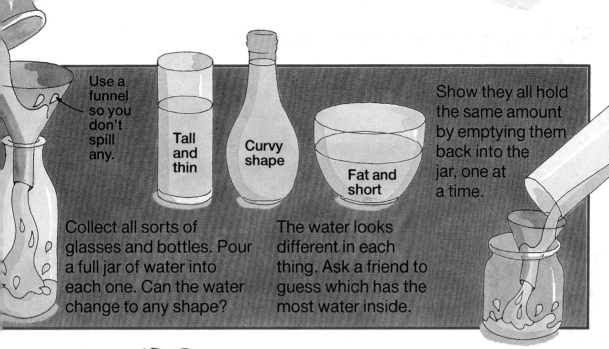

Use a funnel so you don't spill any.

Tall and thin

Curvy shape

Fat and short

Show they all hold the same amount by emptying them back into the jar, one at a time.

Collect all sorts of glasses and bottles. Pour a full jar of water into each one. Can the water change to any shape?

The water looks different in each thing. Ask a friend to guess which has the most water inside.

Rest the bottle on books to keep it steady.

Level top

Sloping bottle

Level table

What do you think will happen if you tilt the bottle? Can you make the top of the water slope? Try it and see. Check the top against a level table.

Now bend a clear plastic tube* into a U-shape. Hold it under a tap to get water inside. Is the top of the water at the same height (level) on both sides?

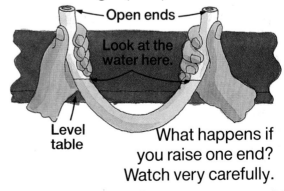

Open ends

Look at the water here.

Level table

What happens if you raise one end? Watch very carefully.

*You can buy this cheaply from a hardware shop.

3

Floating

Some things float on water while others sink.

Which things float?

Collect some things to test for floating. Can you guess which ones float before you put them in water?

Make a chart to show your results.

Look at the things that float. Are they all light? Are any of them big? Do they all float in the same way?

Can you guess what happens if you fix a thing that floats to one that sinks?

Underwater floating

Fix some plasticine to a cocktail stick to make it float upright. Add more until it sinks.

Take off a little at a time. Can you make the stick float just under the surface?

Pushing power

Try pushing a blown-up balloon into a bucket of water. It is hard to do. The water seems to push back.

What happens if you let go?

See how the water rises up the bucket as the balloon pushes it aside.

4

Changing shape

Drop a ball of plasticine in some water. Does it float?

Flatten the ball and shape it like a boat with high sides. Does it float now?

Make the sides higher if it sinks.

Testing shapes

Why does the plasticine float when you change its shape? Try this to help you find out.

Use a felt-tip pen to mark the water-level in a glass of water.

Use a wide glass.

Drop in a ball of plasticine. The water rises a little as the ball pushes it aside. Mark the new level.

First water-level

New water-level

Shape the ball into a boat and float it on the water. Why does the level rise higher?

Level for boat
Level for ball

First water-level

How it works

The boat-shape takes up a bigger space than the ball so it pushes more water aside.

The same amount of plasticine takes up more space.

The more water is pushed aside, the more it pushes back. It pushes the boat so hard that it floats.

Metal ships

Metal ships are very heavy. They are shaped so they push away a lot of water. The water pushes back hard enough to keep the ship afloat.

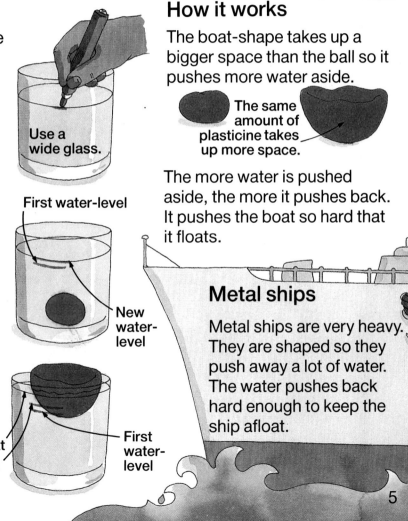

5

Fun with boats

Boats float so well that they can carry heavy things across water.

Everything that a boat carries is called its cargo.

Loading boats

Think of some things which might make good boats. You can see some here. Try them out on water.

Load your boats with a cargo of stones or marbles. Can some carry more than others?

Margarine tub boat

Boat shaped from foil.

Matchbox boat

Is it easier to push a boat-load of cargo along the ground or on the water? Try it to see.

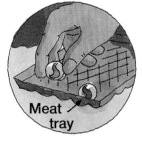

Meat tray

Try loading a plastic meat tray with marbles. What happens?

Load some marbles into a plastic egg box. What happens if you put them all at one end?

Egg box

Try putting one marble in each cup-shape. Does it float better like this?

Cargo ships

Cargo ships have dividing walls inside. This makes sure the cargo cannot move around and tip the ship over.

6

Sinking boat

Stick plasticine under a jar so it floats upright. Mark where the water comes to. Load marbles gently into this boat. What happens to the mark?

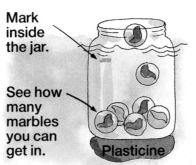

Mark inside the jar.

See how many marbles you can get in.

Plasticine

Put lots of salt in the water. Float the jar now. Does the water come up to the same mark? Can the jar carry more marbles?

Plimsoll line

There are different lines for fresh and salt water.

Plimsoll line

Large boats have marks called Plimsoll lines. People stop loading a boat when the water comes up to this mark.

Submarine can

Push an empty drink can underwater so it fills with water and sinks.

Poke one end of a plastic tube into the can. Blow into the other end. What happens?

The air you blow into the can pushes out the water. This makes the can lighter so it rises to the surface.

Air pocket

Air in

Water out

Submarines

Tanks inside a submarine can be filled with water to make it sink. Air is pumped into the tanks to make the submarine rise again.

Water's 'skin'

Here are some surprises about the top, or surface, of water.

Bulging water

Fill a glass to the brim ▶ with water. Look closely at the top of the water. Gently slide in some coins, one at a time.

Can you see the top rise above the glass?

How many coins can you put in before the water overflows?

Pond skaters

Insects called pond skaters can walk across the top of ponds. They are so light they do not break the water's 'skin'.

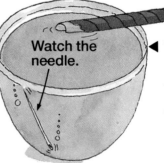

Pond skater

◀ The top of the water seems to bulge as if it is held by a thin skin. The surface of water often behaves like a skin.

Floating a needle

You can float a needle by placing it carefully on the 'skin' like this.

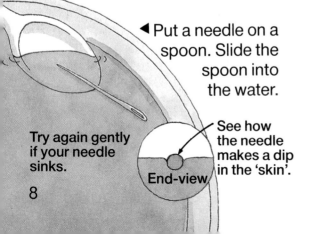

◀ Put a needle on a spoon. Slide the spoon into the water.

Try again gently if your needle sinks.

See how the needle makes a dip in the 'skin'.

End-view

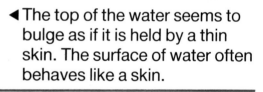

Watch the needle.

◀ What happens if you touch the water with a straw dipped in washing up liquid?

The washing up liquid makes the skin weaker so it stretches. It gets too stretchy to hold up the needle.

Drips and drops

Look out for drops left behind after a rainstorm. Can you guess why water stays in drop shapes?

◀ Try catching a drop from a dripping tap.

Now roll it gently ▶ between your finger and thumb.

What shape are drops as they fall?

Can you change a drop's shape?

All drops are held by water's skin. This holds them even when they change shape.

Flattening drops

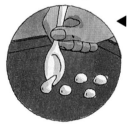

◀ Spoon some drops on to a clean plastic tray. Can you think of a way to make the drops flatter?

Try touching them ▶ with a straw dipped in washing up liquid.

The washing up liquid makes the skin stretch so the drops spread out.

Blowing bubbles

Stir a spoonful of water into three spoonfuls of washing up liquid. This mixture has a very stretchy skin.

Bend some wire into a loop. Dip it in the mixture.

Wire loop

Look at the skin across the loop. Blow gently. Watch how the skin stretches to make a bubble.

9

Vanishing water

You may have noticed how puddles dry up after rain. Have you ever wondered where the water goes?

Finding out

You might think the water just soaks into the ground or runs away. Try an experiment to see if this is true.

Pour some water into a saucer. Use a felt-tip pen to mark a line just above the water.

Leave the saucer on a table for a few days. Look at your mark and the water-level every day.

The water slowly vanishes. It cannot run out or soak through the saucer. It must get out another way.

How water 'vanishes'

The water escapes into the air in tiny drops called water vapour. They are too small to see.

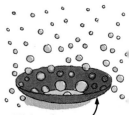

This shows water vapour getting out of a saucer.

This is how a puddle dries up.

Which dries fastest?

Fill three more saucers. Leave one in a cool, shady place, one in a warm place and one in a draughty place. Do they all dry out just as quickly?

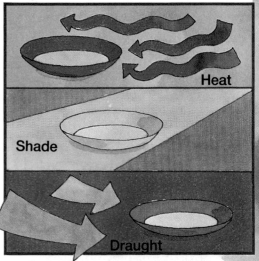

Heat

Shade

Draught

Water in the air

The way water escapes into the air is called evaporation. Water evaporates all the time from rivers and seas so the air is full of invisible water vapour.

Getting water back

Fill a jar with ice-cubes to make it cold. Does anything happen to the outside of the jar?

Wipe it with a dry tissue. Does the tissue get damp?

Put a lid on.

Water drops form on the jar because the cold jar cools the air nearby. When water vapour in the air cools, its drops get big enough to see. This is called condensation.

Steam

Sometimes condensation happens in mid-air. Then the drops look like mist. This happens when water boils.

The water gives off hot water vapour. This cools as it meets colder air and turns to drops you see as steam.

Never touch steam as it can burn you badly.

Clouds and rain

Clouds are also made up of condensation drops. These form when water vapour rises from the ground and meets cold air above.

Drops in the cloud join up and get heavier. Then they fall as rain.

Everlasting seas

Although water evaporates from seas they never dry up. Enough rainwater runs into them to keep them full.

11

Mixing

Water mixes well with many different things. To find out more about the way water mixes, first collect some jars.

Pour some water into each jar. Add a different thing to each one.

You could try:
soap powder,
sand, salt, flour,
sugar, shampoo,
cooking oil,
powder paint,
orange juice,
jelly.

Guess what might happen to each thing before you put it in.

Does anything change if you put the same things into warm water?

Does the colour change?

Put your fingers in to see if the mixtures feel like plain water.

Do any of the things you put in disappear?

Does the water go cloudy or look clear?

Science notebook

Write everything that does happen in your notebook.

Does it make a difference if you stir the mixtures? Watch what happens.

Separating mixtures

Try to think of ways to separate mixtures.

Oil floats so you can scoop it out with a spoon.

Does this work with any other mixtures?

You could use kitchen paper like a fine sieve. First fold the kitchen paper in four. Pull open one side to make a cone.

Oil and water mixture

Put the cone in a funnel. Try pouring the sand mixture into it.

- Bits of sand are trapped.

Water passes through tiny holes in the paper.

Can you separate other mixtures like this?

Solutions

Some things mix so well that you cannot separate them by scooping or sieving. A mixture like this is called a solution.

Separating solutions

Salt water is a solution. Put a drop on a saucer. Leave it until the water evaporates (see pages 10-11).

What is left behind? Taste it and see.*

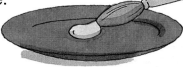

Can you separate other solutions like this?

Instant food

Many foods are partly made of water. Soup, milk and potatoes are often dried and stored as powder.

When people want to eat them they just mix them with water again.

Never taste things unless you know that they are things you can eat. 13

Water power

Water nearly always flows downhill.
Its flow can push things strongly.

Make a model water wheel

You need:
2 plastic egg boxes,
2 small cardboard plates,
a stapler, some scissors,
2 cotton reels, a pencil,
2 long rulers or flat
sticks, plasticine, and
sticky tape.

Can you get the wheel to turn faster?

What happens if you pour from higher up?

How does the water turn the wheel?

Cut cups* out of the egg
boxes. Staple them on to
one plate as shown.
Staple the second plate
on to the other side of
each cup.

Stapler

Push the pencil through
the centre of the plates.
Then push the cotton
reels on to the ends of
the pencil.

Fix the rulers in place
with plasticine.

Tape a ruler below each reel.
Place the rulers across a bowl.
Pour water on the wheel and
watch what happens.

14 *You may not need all the egg-cups.

Powering machinery

Long ago people used water wheels to turn machinery for grinding wheat into flour.

Water mill

Today water is used to power machines that make electricity. The water spins huge wheels called turbines to make these machines work.

Electric generator

Turbine

Electricity is made like this in hydro-electric power stations.

Getting stronger

◄ Take the top off an empty squeezy bottle*. Make three holes in the bottle, one above the other.

Use a ball-point pen.

◄ Tape over the holes. Fill the bottle with water. Then rip the tape off quickly.

Watch how jets of water spurt out. Which goes furthest?

The lowest jet should go furthest as water above it helps to push it out.

*Get an adult to help you take the top off.

Powerful pipes

Pipes to hydro-electric power stations take water from the bottom of lakes or reservoirs. The deeper the pipes are, the faster the water flows along them.

Reservoir

The water spins turbines inside the power station.

Water pipes

Power station

15

Air and water tricks

Most things that look empty are really full of air. Water has to push the air out before it can get in them.

Tissue trick

Do you think you can keep a tissue dry underwater? Try this.

First, stuff the tissue tightly into a glass so it cannot fall out.

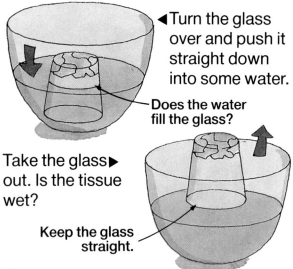

◄Turn the glass over and push it straight down into some water.

Does the water fill the glass?

Take the glass► out. Is the tissue wet?

Keep the glass straight.

This works because the glass is full of air. The water cannot push the air out so the tissue stays dry. What happens if you tilt the glass?

16

Magic pot

Find an empty plastic pot with a tight lid. Use a drawing pin to make holes in its base.

Take off the lid and push the pot underwater. Now put the lid on.

What happens when you lift the pot up?

Air tries to get in the holes. It pushes so hard the water cannot get out.

Does any water fall out?

Now push a ball-point pen through the lid to make another hole. This lets air in at the top. The air helps to push the water out below.

What happens if you put your finger over the hole?

Flowing upwards

Can you make water flow upwards?

1. Stand a glass in the ▶ kitchen sink. Put one end of a plastic tube in the glass. Put the other end under a tap to fill the glass.

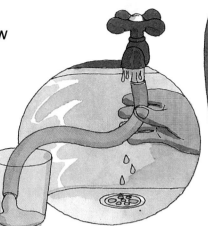

Keep this end underwater.

◀ 2. Put your finger over the top of the tube to keep the water in. Lift the glass up on to the draining board with your other hand.

3. Bend the tube until your finger ▶ is lower than the glass. Take your finger off.

The water should run up out of the glass through the tube. Can you think why?

Keep trying if this does not work first time.

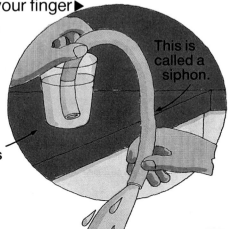

This is called a siphon.

How the siphon works

As water runs out of one end, air pushes more water up the other. This keeps on until all the water has run out.

Air pushes here.

Water is forced up the tube.

Water runs out here.

17

Taking in water

Some things soak up water while others keep water out.

Wetting different things

Put a spoonful of water on a dry sponge. What happens to the water?

Does all the sponge get wet?

Does all the water disappear?

Spoon water on to other things. Make a chart to show what happens to each one.

Do you think water will soak into any of these things?

Which things could you use for mopping up spills? Which might be good for making umbrellas?

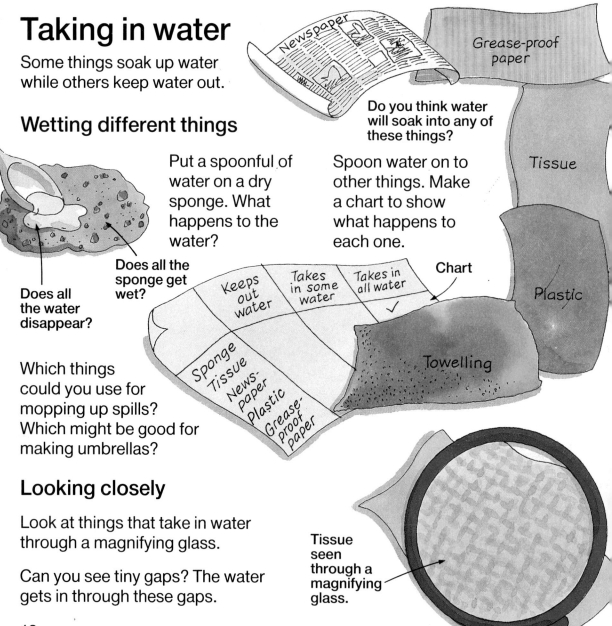

Newspaper

Grease-proof paper

Tissue

Plastic

Chart

	Keeps out water	Takes in some water	Takes in all water
Sponge			
Tissue			✓
Newspaper			
Plastic			
Grease-proof paper			

Towelling

Looking closely

Look at things that take in water through a magnifying glass.

Can you see tiny gaps? The water gets in through these gaps.

Tissue seen through a magnifying glass.

18

Rising water

Do you think water can climb upwards?

Dip a strip of kitchen paper into some water. Watch what happens.

Climbing through celery

Pour a few drops of ink into a glass of water. Cut the end off a stalk of celery. Look at the cut edge closely.

Cut edge

Put the stalk in the water. Leave it for three days. Does anything happen?

What happens to the leaves?

How plants drink

A plant has roots under the earth. These have tiny holes in them.

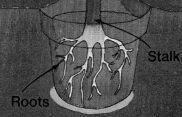

Leaves

Stalk

Roots

Water in the earth goes into the roots. It is sucked up to the leaves through thin tubes in the stalk.

Did you know?

In giant redwood trees, water has to climb one hundred metres to reach the highest leaf.

Inky spots

Cut the stalk into slices. Look for inky spots inside. These show where water has risen up the stalk.

Frozen water

When water gets very cold it freezes hard and turns to ice.

Differences

Look at an ice-cube. How is it different from water?

Can you pour ice like water?

Water can change shape because it is a liquid. Ice keeps one shape unless it melts and turns back to water.

Anything that keeps its shape, like ice, is called a solid.

Taking up space

Find a plastic pot with a lid. Fill it with water and put the lid on. Ask if you can put the pot in a freezer. What happens when all the water turns to ice?

Fill up to the brim.

Ice takes up more space than water. It pushes the lid up when it gets too big for the pot.

Does ice float?

Put some ice in a bowl of water to see if it floats.

How much floats above the surface?

Ships can sink if they hit the hidden part.

Icebergs

Icebergs are huge chunks of ice which float in cold seas. Only the tip can be seen above the water.

Melting ice

Ice melts when it gets warmer.

Guess what happens if you put one ice-cube in cold water, one in hot water and one on a plate.

Try this out to see if you are right.

Use a watch to time how fast they melt.

Melting without heating

Try sprinkling an ice-cube with salt.

What happens to the salt?

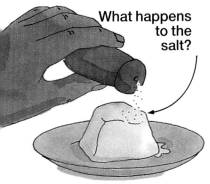

Try pressing an ice-cube with a spoon handle.

What happens to the ice here?

Ice always melts when it is pressed.

The salt mixes with the ice. Salty ice melts quickly because it melts at cooler temperatures than plain ice.

Why ice is slippery

Ice melts when your feet press on it. A thin layer of water forms under your shoes.

This stops them gripping so you slide around.

21

Notes for parents and teachers

These notes give more detailed explanations of the scientific topics covered in this book.

Experimenting with water (pages 2-3)

In common with all liquids, water flows, changes shape to fit any container, keeps the same volume and finds its own level.

Floating (pages 4-5)

When an object is dropped in water its bulk pushes some water aside. The water pushes back, exerting a force called upthrust. If the object is heavy its weight may overcome the upthrust so it sinks. If it is light enough, it floats.

It is possible to make something push aside more water by changing its shape. The boat-shaped plasticine pushes aside more water than the ball. This increases the upthrust so it now keeps the plasticine afloat.

Fun with boats (pages 6-7)

A boat sinks into water until it displaces the same weight of water as its own weight. When loaded, the boat sinks lower into the water until it displaces the weight of its cargo as well as its own weight.

Salt water weighs more than fresh water. A boat has to displace less salt water to equal its own weight. This makes it float higher in salt water. It can also carry more.

Water's 'skin' (pages 8-9)

Like all substances, water is made up of tiny particles called molecules. Water molecules hold together most strongly at the surface. This makes it able to resist slight pressure, just like a skin. This effect is known as surface tension.

The surface molecules attract each other.

Vanishing water (pages 10-11)

Molecules move constantly in a liquid. They often break free and escape as gas (evaporation). Heat gives molecules more energy so they move faster and break free more easily.

▼

Escaping molecules

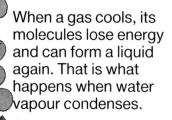

Heat

When a gas cools, its molecules lose energy and can form a liquid again. That is what happens when water vapour condenses.

Mixing (pages 12-13)

Water forms different mixtures with various other substances.

Solutions

A solution is formed when a substance, such as salt, dissolves in water. Its molecules spread out among the water molecules so they are thoroughly mixed.

Suspensions and emulsions

A suspension is formed when a powdery substance, such as fine sand, does not dissolve. Its particles stay large enough to see. They can be easily filtered out.

A liquid, such as oil, that refuses to mix with water can form an emulsion. It stays in droplets suspended in the water.

Water power (pages 14-15)

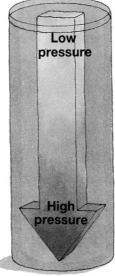

Low pressure

High pressure

Water flows downwards due to gravity (Earth's pull). The force of its flow is useful for powering machinery.

Its flow is also affected by its depth. The deepest parts of any volume of water are under the most pressure because of the weight of water above.

Air and water tricks (pages 16-17)

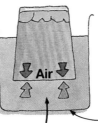

Air

Water

When a glass is pushed underwater, air is trapped inside. The air pressure balances the water pressure outside.

The water compresses the air but cannot push past it.

Taking in water (pages 18-19)

Water molecules can be more attracted to other substances than they are to each other. The attraction enables water to travel a long way into some substances. This is called capillary action.

Capillary action encourages water to climb up plants. Plants allow water to evaporate from their leaves which also helps to 'suck' the water up.

Frozen water (pages 20-21)

When water becomes very cold the molecules lock together to form a solid (ice). Heat gives the molecules energy so they can break free and change to liquid. This also happens if pressure is applied.

Index

air, 11, 16, 17, 22, 23
amount, 3

boats, 5, 6, 7, 22
bubbles, 9

cargo ships, 6
charts, 4, 18
clouds, 11
condensation, 11, 22

drops, 9

electricity, 15
evaporation, 10-11, 22

floating, 4-5, 6-7, 8, 22

hydro-electric power
    stations, 15

ice, 11, 20-21, 22
icebergs, 20
instant foods, 13

level, 2, 3, 22
liquid, 20, 22

melting, 20, 21
metal ships, 5
mixing, 12-13, 23

plants, 19, 23
Plimsoll lines, 7
pond skater, 8
power, 14-15, 23

rain, 10, 11

salt water, 7, 13, 22
science notebook, 2, 12

scientist, 2
seas, 11
separating mixtures, 13
shape, 2, 3, 5, 20, 22
siphon, 17
solid, 20
solutions, 13
steam, 11
submarines, 7
surface, 2, 8

taking in water, 18-19
turbines, 15

underwater, 4, 7

water's 'skin', 8-9, 22
water vapour, 10, 11, 22
water wheels, 14-15

First published in 1990 by Usborne Publishing Ltd, Usborne House, 83-85 Saffron
Hill, London, EC1N 8RT, England. Copyright © 1990 Usborne Publishing Ltd.